A Note for Parents and Teachers

A focus on phonics helps beginning readers gain
skill and confidence with reading. Each story in the
Bright Owl Books series highlights one vowel sound—
for *Blues for Unicorn,* it's the long "u" sound. At the end
of the book, you'll find two Story Starters, just for fun.
Story Starters are open-ended questions that can be
used as a jumping-off place for conversation,
storytelling, and imaginative writing.

At Kane Press, we believe the most important part
of any reading program is the shared experience of
a good story. We hope you'll enjoy *Blues for Unicorn*
with a child you love!

For information regarding permission, contact the publisher through its website: www.kanepress.com

Library of Congress Cataloging-in-Publication Data
Names: Coxe, Molly, author, illustrator.
Title: Blues for unicorn / by Molly Coxe.
Description: New York : Kane Press, [2019] | Series: Bright Owl books |
Summary: "Unicorn and Mule want to start a cool blues group, but Unicorn decides she gets to make all the rules"— Provided by publisher.
Identifiers: LCCN 2018028531 (print) | LCCN 2018035242 (ebook) | ISBN 9781635921113 (ebook) | ISBN 9781635921106 (pbk) | ISBN 9781635921090 (reinforced library binding)
Subjects: | CYAC: Rules (Philosophy)--Fiction. | Blues (Music)--Fiction. | Musicians--Fiction. | Mules--Fiction. | Unicorns--Fiction.
Classification: LCC PZ7.C839424 (ebook) | LCC PZ7.C839424 Rul 2019 (print) | DDC [E]--dc23
LC record available at https://lccn.loc.gov/2018028531

10 9 8 7 6 5 4 3 2 1

First published in the United States of America in 2019
by Kane Press, Inc.
Printed in China

Book Design: Michelle Martinez

Bright Owl Books is a registered trademark
of Kane Press, Inc.

Visit us online at www.kanepress.com

 Like us on Facebook
facebook.com/kanepress

Follow us on Twitter
@KanePress

BLUES FOR
UNICORN

by Molly Coxe

Kane Press • New York

Mule and Unicorn
play music.

"I play the blues," says Unicorn.
"Me too!" says Mule.

"Let's start a blues group!"
says Mule.
"Cool!" says Unicorn.

"We can call it
Unicorn and Mule's
Blues Group," says Mule.
"Super!" says Unicorn.

"I will toot the bugle,"
   says Mule.
"No bugles!"
   says Unicorn.
"Bugles aren't cool."

"I will toot the flute,"
says Mule.
"No flutes!" says Unicorn.

"I will toot the tuba,"
says Mule.
"No tubas!"
says Unicorn.

"No bugle?
No flute?
No tuba?"
says Mule.
"You made up those rules."

"Unicorns always make the rules,"
says Unicorn.
"Unicorns are unique!"

"I am unique, too!"
says Mule.
"Toodaloo, Unicorn!"

Mule starts a new group,
Mule and the Blues Birds.

Mule toots the flute,
the bugle,
and the tuba.
"Who needs rules?
Not mules!"
sing the Blues Birds.

Mule
and the
Blues Birds

Unicorn fumes.
"Mule is not cool!
He is too rude!"

But Unicorn knows
it's not true.
She feels blue.

She writes a tune,
"Blues for Mule."

"No more rules,"
says Unicorn.
"Duet?" asks Mule.

"I am truly blue
without you,"
croon Mule and Unicorn
and two bluebirds, too!

Story Starters

Tell a story
about Mule and Unicorn's
cool canoe.

Sing a tune
to the moon
with Bluebird.